Yada Yada Hi Dharmasya Glanir Bhavati Bharata
Abhyuttanam Adharmasya Tadatnaman Srjamy Aham

Whenever and wherever a decline of righteousness and a
predominance of unrighteousness prevail; at that time
I manifest Myself, O descendant of Bharata

Sri Krishna to Arjuna, Bhagvad Gita, Chapter 4, Verse 7

To Nagendra – with gratitude

For a journey worth its while

For ten years together

And to many more miles....

anJana
publishing

Second Edition, June 2015

House L, Orient Crest, 76 Peak Road, The Peak, Hong Kong

ISBN: 978-988-12394-3-3

Designed by Jump Web Services Ltd.
Production by Macmillan Production (Asia) Ltd.
Tracking Code CP-06/15
Printed in Guangdong Province China
This book is printed on paper made from well-managed sustainable forest sources.

Amma, Tell Me About Krishna!

Part I in the Krishna Trilogy

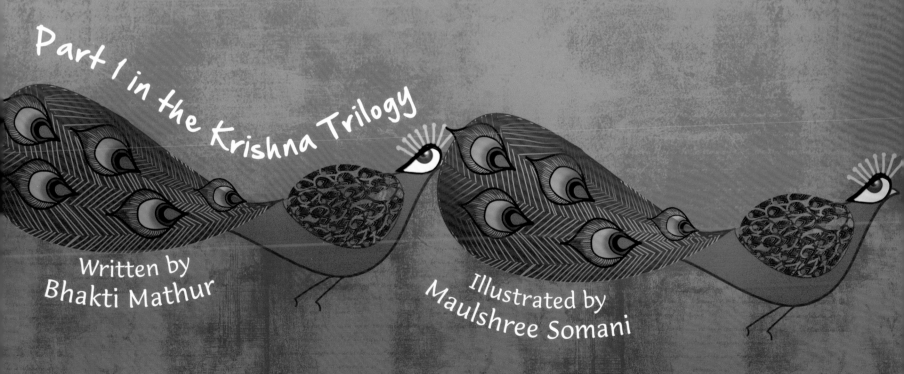

Written by
Bhakti Mathur

Illustrated by
Maulshree Somani

One by one the boys climbed
Forming a pyramid firm and tall,
Till they reached the small earthen pot,
Hanging high up from the temple wall.

Klaka was last to go and carefully he climbed,
His reaching the top was now all that mattered.
He made it and then, a mighty swing of his stick,
And there! The little earthen pot was shattered.

A loud cheer rose from the watching crowd,
The temple erupted with joy and mirth.
For this tradition is a highlight of 'Janamashtami',
The festival that celebrates Krishna's birth!

Klaka and Kiki had barely slept the night before.
For weeks they had looked forward to this day.
They reached the temple early in the morning,
So much to do - a bit of work, but mostly play.

They had helped paint the marks
Of tiny feet on the floor, as though
Baby Krishna himself had walked
Into this very temple, not long ago!

They then helped bathe an idol
Of baby Krishna in fresh milk;
Placed it in a golden cradle,
Dressed in beautiful yellow silk.

One by one, Klaka and his friends
Took turns to rock the cradle gently,
By pulling a string attached to it
Lovingly and ever so carefully.

Finally, the hour of Krishna's birth arrived;
The temple bells tolled to strike midnight.
Many broke out in songs of Krishna's glory,
While others danced to show their delight.

After the festivities were over,
As Amma tucked Klaka into bed,
"I'm not sleepy at all, Amma,
Tell me about Krishna!" he said.

"All right, then listen carefully," said Amma.
"My grandmother used to tell me this story
About how Krishna was born,
Of his great deeds and his rise to glory.

Krishna was born on the monsoon's eight day.
And that is when every year we celebrate
His birthday, which is called 'Janamashtami'.
For 'Janam' means birth and 'Ashtami' means eight.

A long, long time ago, terror had come
To the once-great kingdom of Mathura,
Ever since evil Kansa usurped the crown
From his father, the noble King Ugrasena.

There was fear everywhere,
Destruction, death and pain.
No good citizen was safe
Under wicked Kansa's evil reign.

Desperate, the people turned to the god, Vishnu;
Prayed to him to bring Kansa's reign to an end.
Vishnu heard their prayer and thus proclaimed -
"To end Kansa's rule, to earth I will descend."

Soon after, as Kansa's sister, Devaki,
Was wedded to the noble King Vasudev,
A stroke of lightning flashed through the sky,
And a voice spoke out a prophecy so grave.

"Listen, O wicked Kansa,
Know now that your end is near.
The eight child of Devaki will kill you
And rid Mathura of your reign of fear."

On hearing this, Kansa seized Devaki.
Drew his sword and raised it to kill her.
"My end will never come," he said,
"If I kill you now, my little sister."

Vasudev pleaded with him.
"Kansa, spare your sister's life," he said.
"I promise I will hand you our children;
Do with them what you please instead."

Kansa agreed, but had Devaki and Vasudev
Chained and locked up in a dark prison cell.
Their first seven children were taken on birth;
For the poor parents, it was like time in hell.

Finally, it was time for the eight child's birth,
But, what were Devaki and Vasudev to do?
Kansa had doubled the guards on watch.
How, but how, could the prophecy come true?

Then on the monsoon's eighth day
At the very stroke of midnight.
A beautiful baby boy was born to Devaki,
Lighting up the prison with a godly light.

A divine voice rang out and said,
"Vasudev, your troubles are at an end.
Take this child across the Yamuna river,
To Gokul, where lives Nand, your friend."

Lo and behold, Vasudev's chains came undone
The prison locks fell open on their own stead.
The guards fell to the ground in a deep sleep;
A light appeared to mark Vasudev's path ahead.

In wonder, he picked up the baby
And walked out into the stormy night.
He reached the Yamuna, but how could he cross?
How could he follow the magical light?

He held up the baby over his head,
Bravely stepped forward and then had a shock.
For suddenly, the mighty Yamuna parted,
Revealing a path on which he could walk.

From the river emerged a huge serpent -
The heavenly Shesh Naag, whose giant head
Formed an umbrella over father and son,
As through the parted Yamuna, they tread.

Vasudev reached Nand's house and found
A new born girl lying next to Yashoda, Nand's wife.
He picked up the girl and lay his son in her place,
And as he left, he prayed for the boy's safe life.

Vasudev took the baby girl back to Devaki;
The guards awoke with the baby's cries.
They ran to Kansa with the news of the birth
And he rushed there to see it with his own eyes.

He snatched the baby from Devaki, and
Flung her against the wall with a screech.
But the baby instead flew out of his grip,
Floating up in the air and out of his reach.

The baby was really the Goddess Yogamaya,
And as she flew away, she laughed and said,
"O Kansa, Devaki's eighth child is alive and well
Nothing can save you, you will soon be dead."

Mad with rage, Kansa ordered his soldiers
To seek out all newborns far and wide.
But, Devaki's eight child was safe in Gokul,
Kansa's efforts to find him were all denied.

When Yashoda awoke the next morning,

She took the sleeping boy to be her son.

She fell deeply in love with him that instant,

Naming him Krishna - one who attracts everyone!

Indeed, baby Krishna turned out to be so,
Casting a spell on all who set eyes on him.
The villagers of Gokul rejoiced in his birth,
Ready to pander to his every whim.

So that, my dear Klaka and Kiki,

Is the story of how Krishna came to be.

Wait for another time to find out whether

He could fulfil the divine prophecy."